The Tree

by *Karen Gray Ruelle*

illustrated by

Deborah Durland DeSaix

Holiday House / *New York*

With all my love to Lee and Nina
& to my dear friend Deb, who planted the seed for The Tree
K. G. R.

For George, with all my heart; and for Karen, my dearest friend
and a great writer. Am I ever lucky!
D. D. D.

Author's Note

It is impossible to know for certain the origins of a 250-year-old English elm tree growing in the middle of New York City. While there are a number of possibilities, I have chosen to show just one.

Acknowledgments

Many thanks to the librarians, historians, arborists, and others who helped me in my research, especially: Chris Roddick, head arborist at the Brooklyn Botanic Garden; Kim Wickers, director of horticulture at Madison Square Park; Dorey Rosen at the New York Botanical Garden; Stuart Desmond, Madison Square Conservancy; Katherine Powis, librarian at the Horticultural Society of New York; Samuel Bishop and Joe Bernardo at Trees NY; John Mattera, New York City Parks Department librarian; Jonathan Kuhn, New York City Parks Department historian; Benjamin Swett; Mike Feller, New York City Parks Department Natural Resources Group; and Nancy Kandoian and Alice Hudson, Map Room librarians at the New York Public Library. And many thanks also to Miriam Berman for her splendid book *Madison Square*.

The text typeface is Garamond #3.
The artwork for this book was created with watercolor as well as oil paint rubbed with paper towels.
www.holidayhouse.com
First Edition
1 3 5 7 9 10 8 6 4 2

Library of Congress Cataloging-in-Publication Data
Ruelle, Karen Gray.
The tree / by Karen Gray Ruelle ; illustrated by Deborah Durland DeSaix. — 1st ed.
p. cm.
Summary: Recounts the life of an elm tree from the time it falls to the ground as a seed, through its growth while momentous events occur to humans and their city, to its maturity as the oldest tree in the park, spreading its canopy for all to enjoy.
ISBN-13: 978-0-8234-1904-3 (hardcover)
ISBN-10: 0-8234-1904-5 (hardcover)
[1. Elm—Fiction. 2. Trees—Fiction.] I. DeSaix, Deborah Durland, ill. II. Title.
PZ7.R88525Tre 2009
[E]—dc22
2006002014

It was springtime, and tiny wildflowers were bursting forth all along the creek. Field mice scampered through the grasses, searching for seeds to eat. Chipmunks were stuffing their cheeks with nuts in the shade of an elm tree. Suddenly a strong breeze shook the branches of the tree and a shower of seedpods came loose. They danced in the air, then slowly spiraled to the ground.

A chipmunk grabbed one of the pods and nearly ran off with her prize; but then there was another breeze, the warning rush of air that comes from beating wings. A red-tailed hawk swooped down from the tree from which it had been watching. The chipmunk dashed off into her burrow. In her haste she dropped the seedpod.

That night it rained. It was a steady rain that soaked the ground, making it muddy and soft. The seed-pod settled into the squishy mud.

1686
Land set
aside as
public space

The sun rose the next morning, and it was a glorious day. That evening the seed in the pod began to take root. The tiny rootlet reached slowly downward. Earthworms had burrowed underneath it and churned up fertile soil. The root continued to reach deep into the ground. It held fast throughout the rest of the spring and summer, as a network of roots channeled through the earth.

In time the seed split open and a little leafed stem unfurled itself. Nourished by rain and sun and the rich soil underneath, a tiny elm tree was born.

1756
Seedpod
sprouts

Autumn came. The days grew shorter and the nights grew longer. The wind blew hard, shaking the leaves from the trees. A pile of brown leaves settled on top of the seedling, protecting it from foraging animals and birds.

Snow fell. Chipmunks slept in their burrows. Squirrels scrambled and searched for food. Deer gnawed on the bark of a nearby tree and pawed the ground. A fox crept silently past, looking for a meal. It pounced on a mole that had emerged near the seedling and knocked over a small stone. The stone fell onto the seedling, which remained hidden for the rest of the winter.

Spring drizzle thawed the snow mounds and made currents in the muddy earth. One strong current carried away the stone that covered the seedling. Now it was bared to the bright, bright sun.

The tiny sprout grew quickly and soon became a sapling. Before too long the sapling was a tall, strong tree, overlooking a nearby roadway and the farm beyond.

Years passed, and one day the land around the tree was cleared of rocks and other trees to make room for a potter's field. The rats that came there ran right past the tree. They frightened away the chipmunks and squirrels. So did the people who came to bury their dead. The desolate field looked pitted and sad. Stones marked the graves of the many victims of yellow fever. Soon there were so many stone markers, no more would fit. People stopped coming. Weeds and grasses grew around the stones and around the tree.

1794
Yellow fever
Potter's field

When the grasses had filled in most of the field, the squirrels and chipmunks returned, and so did field mice; but they were soon frightened away again. First the land was plowed and planted with corn. Then soldiers arrived. They built an arsenal for their weapons and they marched. Their heavy boots pounded the ground and their gunshots rang in the air. The tree stood proud and tall, mostly undisturbed. From time to time a soldier might stop to lean back against its trunk. A soldier might practice a shot or two, using the tree as a target; but the wounds in its bark healed.

1806–1814
Military
arsenal and
parade ground
created

1814
Named
Madison
Square

The tree's trunk had become thick, and its branches were filled with leaves. The soldiers were gone now. In their place were children who sometimes climbed the tree. Children who might carve their initials into the bark. Soon, though, there was a terrible fire, and then no more children came to the tree. The wind blew the smoke away, but nearly everything was burned to the ground. The tree was left on a charred piece of land. Even the creek that had once flowed nearby was one. It had become an underground waterway.

1825–1839
Home for
children
in former
arsenal

1839
Home for
children
destroyed
in fire

In time the wild grasses grew back around the tree. Chipmunks and squirrels scampered back to the tree, and birds came to perch on its branches once again. They were not the only animals there. Pigs wandered through the city's parks and squares, eating garbage and leaving behind their own waste. There were times when a baseball from a neighboring field would sail through the air and get caught up in the tree's branches. Not far away, horses hauled train cars along iron tracks back and forth from the depot. Meanwhile, at the inn at the crossroads nearby, a steady stream of stagecoaches came and went, dropping off weary travelers and picking up others. The land around the tree became a city park, its borders defined by fences, brownstones lining the streets around it. Then there was a war, and for a time the park was filled with the tents of soldiers.

1830–1860
New York
and Harlem
Rail Road
depot

1840–1856
Former
farmhouse
becomes
Madison
Cottage Inn

1845
Knickerbocker
Base Ball Club
field opens

In the park, new trees grew tall alongside the first tree. After a while a huge building rose nearby. It was filled with horses and other circus animals. Parades of elephants thundered across the field, stopping sometimes to rub their itchy backs against the strong trunk of the towering tree. Circus horses galloped around the tree, rested in its shade, and grazed on the grass beneath it. Birds made their nests in the tree, and a family of squirrels lived in its boughs.

1873–1879
Circus at
P. T. Barnum's
Hippodrome

For a time the tree was joined by a towering piece of a statue: an arm holding a torch. People stood back to marvel at the statue, and some climbed ladders up to the torch. Sometimes they clambered up the tree to get a better look at the statue. They still had to look up.

1876–1882
Statue of
Liberty arm
and torch
on display

When the elephants and the horses left, more people came. They arrived in huge crowds from time to time, chanting, singing, marching, applauding, laughing, crying, playing. More fences were built around the tree and its land. By now the tree was so huge, it became a meeting place, a landmark. Other trees grew around it, but it was the tallest, the strongest, the leafiest.

1889–1920
Parades,
celebrations,
political
demonstrations,
and riots

Around the tree, the city grew. Grand houses, elegant hotels, and concert halls gave way to skyscrapers and apartment buildings. Other trees grew beside the tree. Then there was a disease that killed many of the trees. The leafy elm survived, and people came to admire it and to picnic in its shade.

After a while, as times changed, people no longer came to sit under the tree. It was a troubled time in the city. But with the passage of the years, people slowly started coming back. The tree, now the oldest one there, spread its enormous canopy of branches and leaves over the city park.

1930s
Dutch elm
disease strikes

1960s–1980s
Park falls
into disrepair

1986–2001
Restoration
of park

Birds still nest in the old
tree's branches, but time has worn
down the reach of its leafy limbs.
Squirrels still live in a hollow in its
massive trunk. In the ground below,
among its ancient roots, chipmunks
still burrow. Who knows, perhaps one
day, on a beautiful spring morning
when the wind is blowing hard, a
shower of seedpods will fall from
the tree and land on the pavement
below. Perhaps a little chipmunk
will scurry over and pick one up
in her paws. Then a woolly dog on
the nearby pathway may see the
chipmunk and may bark at her.
Perhaps the chipmunk will drop
the seed on the ground and scamper
away. Maybe right now—this
very moment—there is a tiny seed
beginning to take root in the ground
near the great, old elm tree.

1997
150th anniversary
of Madison
Square Park

2006
The tree is
250 years old

Historical Notes

In 1686 the area now known as Madison Square Park in New York City was rocky, swampy land surrounded by a small stream called Cedar Creek. That year, Thomas Dongan, royal governor of New York, set aside the land as public space. Over the years more land was added until the park reached the 6.8 acres it is today.

By the 1700s the area was surrounded by farmland. Two roads met there. One led to Albany, New York, and the other went right through the park area to Boston. A farmhouse by this busy intersection, called Madison Cottage, became a post tavern for weary travelers to change their horses or spend the night.

Sometime around 1756 an English elm tree seedpod (called a samara) fell to the ground, and a day or two later it began to take root.

In 1794 there was the first in a series of yellow fever outbreaks, which claimed many lives. To accommodate the

bodies of immigrants, paupers, and those who could not be buried in a regular cemetery, the park area was turned into a potter's field. It was completely filled in three years and the remains were moved to another site. Some time later the stone markers were moved and the land was plowed and planted with corn. Common Council decreed in 1807 that part of the land be set aside as a public square forever.

The land was used for target practice in the 1800s. In 1806 a military arsenal was built, and the following year the area became a parade ground for practicing military maneuvers. Soldiers prepared there for the War of 1812. President James Madison was in his second term in 1814. The parade ground was named Madison Square in his honor.

In 1823 the arsenal was abandoned and the land became the property of the city of New York. Then, in 1825,

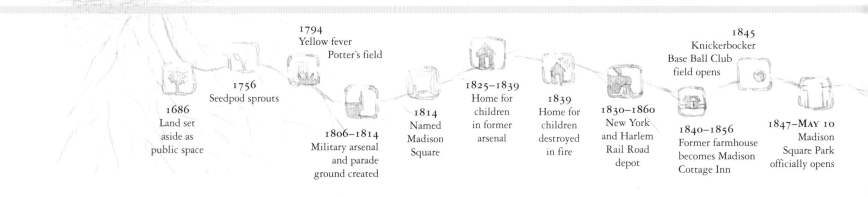

1686
Land set
aside as
public space

1756
Seedpod sprouts

1794
Yellow fever
Potter's field

1806–1814
Military arsenal
and parade
ground created

1814
Named
Madison
Square

1825–1839
Home for
children
in former
arsenal

1839
Home for
children
destroyed
in fire

1830–1860
New York
and Harlem
Rail Road
depot

1840–1856
Former farmhouse
becomes Madison
Cottage Inn

1845
Knickerbocker
Base Ball Club
field opens

1847–May 10
Madison
Square Park
officially opens

a House of Refuge was set up in the arsenal for juvenile delinquents, orphans, and children whose parents were in jail or in asylums. By the end of the first year it housed more than a thousand children and became an institution so famous that British author Charles Dickens came to visit it. At that time Madison Square was on the outskirts of town surrounded by farms and orchards. The House of Refuge burned nearly to the ground in 1839. The land became muddy and swampy again and was a popular place for children to play.

New York City's main railroad, the New York and Harlem Rail Road, built a station at Madison Avenue and Twenty-sixth Street, right by the park, in 1832. The area became busy with travelers.

By 1844 Madison Square Park was very much the same as it is today, with one addition: pigs. At that time pigs roamed the parks, gardens, and the streets of the city. They were there to eat the trash, but unfortunately they made more of a mess than they cleaned up. In 1845 New York's first baseball team, the Knickerbocker Base Ball Club, organized a playing field just next to the park.

The ground in Madison Square Park was leveled, sodded, and enclosed by a fence. On May 10, 1847, the renovated Madison Square Park was officially reopened.

In 1859 Amos Eno opened the Fifth Avenue Hotel next to the park on the site of the old Madison Cottage. It was considered to be so far uptown that it was dubbed "Eno's Folly." However, the area soon became the center of a fashionable neighborhood, and for the next fifteen years, the Fifth Avenue Hotel remained the largest hotel in the

world. It became the headquarters of the Republican Party, while the headquarters of the Democratic Party was right nearby at Hoffman House. Madison Square was at one end of Ladies' Mile, a popular street of upscale shops and restaurants. Many celebrities lived in the neighborhood, including Theodore Roosevelt, Jennie Jerome (the mother of Winston Churchill), and novelists Edith Wharton, Herman Melville, and Henry James.

During the Civil War, many of New York's parks became campgrounds for soldiers. Madison Square was filled with tents.

In 1870 the newly organized Department of Public Parks took control of Madison Square. They placed iron railings around the park and planned a renovation.

Throughout the years Madison Square Park has been the site of celebrations, exhibitions, and demonstrations. At the centennial of the signing of the Declaration of Independence in 1876, there was a big celebration in the park. In the 1870s a portion of the Statue of Liberty was put on display in the park to help raise money to build the base of the statue. The arm holding a torch aloft stood in the park, and for 50 cents, visitors could climb a ladder up to its balcony.

After the train station moved uptown to its current location at Grand Central Terminal, P. T. Barnum leased the depot to house his circus. Rodeos and the annual circus were held at Barnum's Hippodrome. In 1879 the Barnum group bought the building and converted it into the first Madison Square Garden. The building continued to be

1860–1865
Civil War military campgrounds

1873–1879
Circus at P. T. Barnum's Hippodrome

1876–1882
Statue of Liberty arm and torch on display

1889–1920
Parades, celebrations, political demonstrations, and riots

1930s
Dutch elm disease strikes

1960s–1980s
Park falls into disrepair

1986–2001
Restoration of park

1997
150th anniversary of Madison Square Park

2006
The tree is 250 years old

used for the circus, rodeos, horse shows, livestock shows, dog shows, and other events.

Ten years later the depot was demolished and a new Madison Square Garden was built. This building was designed by architect Stanford White. It was the second tallest building in New York City and had the largest auditorium in the country. It also housed a theater, a concert hall, apartments, a roof cabaret, and the city's largest restaurant. Madison Square Garden remained there until 1926, when it moved to the west side of the city.

In 1892 there was a celebration held in the park for the 400th anniversary of Columbus's voyage to America. In 1889 there were three days of parades and a celebration in the park to commemorate the centennial anniversary of George Washington's presidential inauguration. The Fourth of July brought fireworks displays to the park.

With all the politicians nearby, the park became a center for political speeches and demonstrations. It is said that the term "stump speech" originated in a politician's speech made standing on a tree stump in Madison Square Park. In the days before television, the park was also the place to be on election night, as election results were projected onto the side of a nearby building.

In 1902 one of the most famous buildings in New York was built across from the south end of the park. The Flatiron Building has a thin triangular shape, somewhat like the jutting prow of a ship.

For many years, beginning in 1912, a huge Christmas tree was erected and decorated in the park each year.

The early 1900s were a time of great unrest. There were many riots and demonstrations in the park during this period. By the 1930s, fences were erected around the park to help control the crowds of rabble-rousers.

Through the 1930s, elm trees in this country died from Dutch elm disease, which is caused by a fungus and is spread by bark beetles. The elm, once a common tree, became quite rare.

From the mid to late twentieth century, the park fell into disrepair. During this period, many people avoided the park as it became a hangout for petty criminals and other unsavory characters. Then a complete restoration of the park began in 1986. By the time of the park's 150th anniversary in 1997, the northern end of the park had been restored, but the southern end was not restored until the early twenty-first century. Madison Square Park is now restored to its former glory.

Our elm still stands in the middle of the park in New York City. Older than the park by many years, it is a home to squirrels and birds and other park wildlife. It is a witness to all that has gone on around it as the city has grown and changed. The massive elm is now more than 250 years old and, sadly, is reaching the end of its life cycle. Its dying limbs have been removed and now the majestic trunk is all that remains of this proud monument, still standing tall in Madison Square Park.

PiCTURE THiS!

Activities and Adventures in IMPRESSIONISM

by Joseph, 7

JOYCE RAIMONDO

Watson-Guptill Publications/New York

by Paula, 11

Copyright © 2004 by Joyce Raimondo

First published in 2004 by Watson-Guptill Publications
A division of VNU Business Media, Inc.
770 Broadway, New York, N.Y. 10003
www.watsonguptill.com

Step-by-step artwork by Joyce Raimondo. Photographs of three-dimensional art by Rachel Movitz.

Picture credits: Page 9 *Garden at Sainte-Adresse* by Claude Monet. © Artists Rights Society (ARS), New York / ADAGP, Paris. The Metropolitan Museum of Art, purchase, special contributions and funds given or bequeathed by friends of the Museum, 1967 (67.241). Photograph © 1989 The Metropolitan Museum of Art. **Page 19** *The Boulevard Montmartre on a Winter Morning* by Camille Pissarro. The Metropolitan Museum of Art, Gift of Katrin S. Victor, in loving memory of Ernest G. Victor, 1960 (60.174). Photograph © 1990 The Metropolitan Museum of Art. **Page 25** *The Rehearsal Onstage* by Edgar Degas. The Metropolitan Museum of Art, H. O. Havemeyer Collection, Bequest of Mrs. H. O. Havemeyer, 1929 (29.100.39). Photograph © 1989 The Metropolitan Museum of Art. **Page 33** *Dance at the Moulin de la Galette* by Pierre-Auguste Renoir. Copyright © Réunion des Musées Nationaux/Art Resource New York. **Page 39** *The Family* by Mary Cassatt. Chrysler Museum of Art, Norfolk, Virginia, Gift of Walter P. Chrysler, Jr., 71.498.

Library of Congress Cataloging-in-Publication Data

Raimondo, Joyce.
Picture this! : activities and adventures in impressionism /Joyce Raimondo.
    p. cm. —(Art explorers)
  ISBN 0-8230-2503-9 (hardcover : alk.paper)
  1. Impressionism (Art)—Juvenile literature. 2. Impressionism (Art)—Technique—Juvenile literature. 3. Art appreciation—Juvenile literature. I. Title.
    N7432.5.I4R35 2004
    759.05'4—dc22
                        2004007356

Senior Acquisitions Editor: Julie Mazur
Project Editor: Laaren Brown
Designer: Edward Miller
Production Manager: Hector Campbell
The typefaces in this book include Futura, Typography of Coop, and Ad Lib.

Manufactured in Singapore

First printing, 2004

1 2 3 4 5 6 7 / 10 09 08 07 06 05 04

by Bradley, 9

Contents

by Jaclyn, 12

Help Your Child Explore Impressionism

Picture This! invites children to enter the world of Impressionism and use it as a **springboard for their own creativity.** The discussions in this book encourage children to **examine** works of art and **develop their own personal interpretations.** Related projects, inspired by Impressionist concepts, guide children to express themselves.

What do you see in this picture?

The Impressionists wanted to convey the sensations of a place at a particular moment in time. Looking at their pictures, you can imagine a cool breeze blowing on a hot summer day or a crowded dance filled with activity. The questions in this book **motivate creative thinking** by asking children to describe and interpret Impressionist paintings. Let go of your own ideas about what the artwork means and affirm the children's insights. In a group, **encourage different opinions.** Ask children to go further with their ideas. Older children may want to research the artists' lives, and they can start with the brief biographies in this book.

Picture your world

The Impressionists looked to their everyday lives and the world around them for inspiration. They portrayed their family and friends, the places where they traveled, and the life of the city in their art. *Picture This!* invites children to do the same—**to explore their world through art.** Some projects ask children to try working methods of the Impressionists, such as painting with dabs of color. Other projects **explore Impressionist concepts** with materials adapted for children—for example, inspired by Camille Pissarro, children capture weather with sponge painting.

by Cosima, 7

Everyone is creative

The art instructions in this book guide young artists on **a journey of discovery.** Do not expect children to follow them exactly. Begin with a lively conversation to **spark ideas.** For example, discuss Renoir's picture of the dance hall, and ask children about their favorite dances. Then show specific techniques, such as how to draw a person in motion. Sometimes it is helpful to let children **play with the materials**—mixing colors or smudging pastels on a separate paper—before they begin the project. Encourage children to let their art evolve as they work with a spirit of **experimentation.** Keep in mind the developmental level of children. Young children are not interested in painting from direct observation and creating realism. As they paint, they make symbols to represent their world and to tell stories. A young child is happy to paint a person who is as tall as a building or a sun that is a yellow circle. Not until the preadolescent stage do children become interested in creating a realistic look. Remember, **everyone has his or her own way of making things,** and telling children how they should make their art stifles creativity. Celebrate the expressive ideas of the child—creativity is a gift to be nurtured in everyone.

by Allison M., 9

Impressionism and the Art of the Moment

Today Impressionist paintings may look beautiful to us, but in their own time they were a radical departure from what was considered acceptable in art. In the nineteenth century, a group of young painters in Paris broke away from traditional religious, historical, or mythological subjects and turned to their everyday life for inspiration. Rather than painting models inside the atelier, or studio, they established a new way of working: *en plein air*—French for "outdoors." With easels and paints, they traveled to the countryside, the coast, and the city, and painted what they observed on the spot. They painted rapidly with quick brushstrokes to capture the moment and changes in sunlight and weather.

The Impressionists gathered in cafés in Paris to discuss their ideas. Earlier in the century, the city had been transformed with wide boulevards, train stations, and spacious parks, and the Impressionists captured the activity and energy in their art—and they showed both the wealthy and the working classes the way they looked naturally, at work or in their leisure. The availability of photography allowed artists to study the movements of people in a completely new way.

Most of the artists' paintings were rejected from the established exhibition in Paris, the Salon. In 1874, the group organized its first independent exhibition. One of the works on display, by Claude Monet, was called *Impression: Sunrise.* A critic mocked them, calling them "impressionists"—and the group adopted the name. After many years of rejection and struggle, the Impressionists gained critical and financial success. Today, Impressionist paintings are among the world's most beloved treasures of art.

A revolutionary art movement, Impressionism opened the door to abstract painting, marking the beginning of modern art. *Picture This!* highlights five major Impressionists: Claude Monet, Camille Pissarro, Edgar Degas, Pierre-Auguste Renoir, and Mary Cassatt.

Picture Your World

Do you like to play in the snow in the winter, or jump in a pile of colorful leaves in the fall? Isn't it pretty in springtime when flowers bloom? The **world around us is always changing.** What happens where you live each season? What happens throughout the day and night? Isn't it amazing how the sky turns fiery colors at sunset and the stars glisten in the dark? People are always changing and **moving**, too. How do you feel when you are running or dancing or jumping up high? How does your face look when you are happy or sad?

This book invites you to **explore your world** and **capture it in art.** Start with a journey through pictures by **Impressionist** artists. In their paintings, you can travel to the ocean on a hot summer day or take a stroll down a busy city street. You can **step into the paintings** and feel like you are right there.

The Impressionists were a group of artists who met in Paris and became friends. They took trips to the **seashore**, the **countryside**, and the **city**, and they painted what they saw. They painted quickly with dabs of **colors** to show the **sunlight** and **weather**. The Impressionists tried to sell their paintings in the important art exhibition in Paris, called the Salon. But the judges didn't like their work and most of the art was rejected. So the artists put on their own art shows. After years of hard times, their work began to sell, and today they are known as **great artists.**

by Thomas, 7

See for yourself. **Look** at their paintings and **make up stories** about them. Then **create your own art.** Paint a colorful garden or a sunset at the seashore. Notice the world around you—and **let your imagination run free!**

by Dezaray, 11

by Victoria, 10

Play with Color

Like the Impressionists, paint and discover what kinds of colors you can make. To start, set up your paints in rainbow order—red, orange, yellow, green, blue, purple—then brown and white. (The Impressionists did not use black because they liked bright paintings.) Mix colors on an artist's palette or a plastic plate. As you paint, wash your paintbrushes in clean water, and wipe them with a sponge or paper towel.

Make a color wheel. Start with **primary colors**: red, blue, and yellow. Mix two primaries in equal amounts to make **secondary colors**. For example, blue and yellow make green. Then mix any two colors together to make **tertiary colors.** For instance, a touch of red and lots of yellow make yellow-orange.

Experiment. Mix cool colors. Blues, greens, and purples are cool like water and a winter sky. **Mix warm colors.** Reds, oranges, and yellows are warm like the sun or fire. **Mix tints.** Make any color lighter by adding white. **Mix opposites.** Make a color duller by adding the color opposite it on the color wheel. For example, green and red make a brownish color.

7

COLOR MY WORLD

CLAUDE MONET

Claude Monet loved to set up his easel outside and paint his pictures right on the spot. This new way of painting was called *en plein air* (French for "outdoors"). Monet spent the summer of 1867 on the coast of France with his family. In this picture, his father and aunt sit watching the water. His cousin, with a parasol, talks to a man wearing a top hat. Everyone seems to be enjoying the beautiful day.

Monet stood above the scene. He painted quickly so he could capture this special moment in time. It is as if we can step right into the picture. Can you feel the warm sun and the cool breeze? Look at the flags blowing and the sailboats gliding in the wind. Monet used dabs of bright colors and lively brushstrokes to capture this sunny seaside scene.

Imagine visiting this place. What would it be like?

- What do you think these people are **doing**?
- Look at their **clothing**. Why are they dressed this way? What are the women **holding**?
- **Where** is this? How would you describe this **place**?
- Can you tell what **country** this is in? Look closely—find a clue in the picture.
- What is the weather like? What in the picture shows it is a **windy day**? How can we tell the **sun** is shining?
- Look out onto the **water**. What kinds of **boats** do you see? What do the boats tell us about the weather? Notice the **waves**. How can we tell they are **moving**?

Garden at Sainte-Adresse, 1867
oil on canvas, 38⅝ x 51⅛ inches
The Metropolitan Museum of Art, New York

- What **season** might this be? How can you tell?
- What **time** do you think it is? (Look at the shadows to get a clue.)
- Notice the beautiful **garden**. What kinds of colors do you see in it?

Would you want to be in the picture? Why or why not?

Paint your own favorite outdoor places.
The art projects in this section invite you to capture the beauty of your world with color and paint.

At the Seaside

Wind and Waves

Make art inspired by Monet

Paint a colorful seaside picture.

Did you ever visit an ocean, a lake, or a river? Sometimes the waves are so huge—it's fun to ride them in! Other times, the water is calm, and you can float on your back. The water is always changing. On sunny days, it sparkles with light. During a storm, it looks dark and gray. Like Monet, capture a moment at the sea. Show the wind, waves, and weather in your picture.

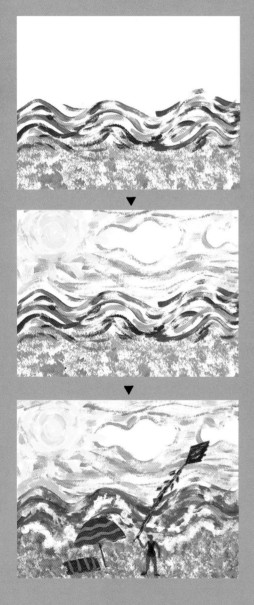

1. Stipple the sand. Dip your brush into paint, then gently dab the tip of the brush straight down onto your painting. Continue to dab the paint around to get the look of grainy sand. You can make sandy colors by mixing orange, white, and touches of red.

2. Paint the waves. Brush on swirling lines for rough waves, or paint straight smooth lines across for calm water. You can make cool colors for water by mixing blue with purple, green, or white.

3. Picture the sky. What is the weather like? Paint a bright sun shining or rain on a cloudy day. Or show a sunset sky made of reds, oranges, and yellows.

4. Catch the wind. Paint curving lines in the sky to show the movement of the breeze. You can also paint flags, kites, and hair blowing, or an umbrella flying in the air!

5. Add finishing touches. Wait for your painting to dry. Then paint or draw people, beach umbrellas, blankets, and other details. You can also paint in fluffy whitecaps for big waves and strokes of color for sparkling reflections on the water.

Supplies

Paper
Brushes
Paint supplies

I understood, I saw, what painting could be! From that moment on my way was decreed. I would be a painter no matter what.—Claude Monet

The sun is setting. —Natalia, 9

Fly a kite! —Jeannette, 7

We're swimming! —Alison, 7

Try these, too!

Painting the Storm

Monet visited the seaside and painted it in all kinds of weather—even during storms! Make your own painting that captures a stormy sea. You might paint a tornado, a lightning storm, a blizzard, a hurricane, or a rain shower. Use brushstrokes to show the movement of the waves, wind, or raindrops. Paint the colors of the sea during the storm.

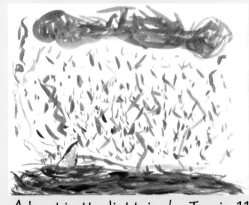

A boat in the lightning! —Travis, 11

Seeing in the Dark

Have you ever visited the beach at night? Sometimes darkness shines with brightness from the stars, moon, and reflections of light on the water. Paint a picture that shows the colors of the seaside at night. You can show **color contrast** by painting bright yellows and whites for stars against dark purples and blues in the sky.

Night light. —Melaina, 11

Sensational Seasons

Make a painting that captures the season.

Have you ever watched snow fall in winter or noticed how leaves change colors in autumn? Sometimes Monet painted the same place many times to show the changing seasons and weather. Like Monet, you can go outside and paint the season, or picture it from your memory.

1. What makes each season special? Here are some ideas: Winter is snowflakes, bare trees, and blizzards. Spring is bright flowers, green grass, and cool breezes. Summer is hot sunshine, blue skies, and beaches. Autumn is leaves that change colors and fall from trees.

2. Paint with dabs of color and quick brushstrokes. Start with the ground. For spring, I painted slanted brushstrokes to show grass blowing. You might paint patches of colored leaves for autumn or white spots for winter snow.

3. Add trees. Use brushstrokes to create the look of bark on the trunk and branches. Mix red and green to make brown. Add a touch of blue to make it darker or white to make it lighter.

4. Paint colors for leaves or flowers. You can mix different amounts of blue, green, yellow, and white to get colors for leaves. Add reds and other bright colors for flowers. For fall, try mixing yellows, oranges, and reds for leaves.

5. Paint wind and sky. Instead of painting the sky one solid color, use brushstrokes to show the direction of the wind. Choose colors to show the sky in that season. Is the summer sun shining in a bright blue sky? Is it a gray cloudy day, or are snowflakes falling?

6. Add something fun. Show what you like about that time of year—such as pumpkins, snowmen, or anything else you enjoy.

7. Look again! Paint the same place again in a different season.

Supplies

Paper
Brushes
Paint supplies

I made a snowman.—Maria, 11

My neighbors grow spring flowers.
—Joseph, 7

I rake and rake in the fall.—Shannon, 11

The sunset is like a fire!—Allison, 11

Try this, too!

Sunrise, Sunset

Monet painted the same scene at different times of day—at dawn, in the afternoon, and at dusk. Have you ever noticed the beautiful colors of the sky at sunrise or sunset? Make a painting that captures this special time. Try mixing **warm colors**—fiery yellows, oranges, and reds for the sky. Paint the silhouettes of trees or the reflection of the sun on the ocean.

How Does Your Garden Grow?

Create a colorful garden using tissue paper collage.

Monet traveled through France and painted beautiful gardens filled with colorful flowers. When he grew older, he bought a house on a river. He created a spectacular garden on the grounds of his home, and it inspired some of his greatest paintings. Do you have a special garden that you enjoy? Can you imagine one?

1. Draw a garden. Use large shapes and draw lightly. You can draw flowers such as tulips, daisies, sunflowers, or roses. Add leaves, butterflies, or insects.

2. Tear it up! Instead of using paint like Monet, use colored tissue paper for your garden. Start by ripping tissue paper into small pieces.

3. Paste it down. Brush glue onto an area of your paper. Then, place bits of tissue paper down flat onto the glue. Brush over them with a thin layer of glue. (Tips: Before you begin, thin the glue by adding water to it. Glue light-colored tissue first, and then add darker ones, to prevent colors from running. As you work, do not brush glue over the same area too much—it will make the colors run.)

4. Use dabs of color. Do not fill in each shape with one solid color. Instead, paste spots of different colors side by side to create a shimmering look.

5. Layer colors. Create all kinds of new colors by gluing tissue paper pieces on top of one another. For example, if you glue yellow on red, you will get an orange color. Green over blue will give you bluish green. Experiment. See what kinds of colors you can make.

Supplies

Paper
Tissue paper
Glue
Glue brush

Pink roses are pretty!—Julie, 9

We grow tomatoes.—Anthony, 9

Fish swim in my pond.—Christina, 10

Try this, too!

Wonderful Water Lilies

In his garden, Monet created a beautiful pond filled with water lilies. He watched the water lilies floating and the reflection of the sky and grass on the water. Monet made twenty paintings inspired by his water lily pond. Paint your own pond. Mix different blues and greens for the water. Then add tissue paper shapes for fish, flowers, leaves, grass, or anything else you imagine.

Dot to Dot

Try pointillism!

Paint an outdoor scene with dots of color.

Look at Monet's garden on page 9. Notice how it is painted with spots of greens, yellows, and reds. Other artists, Camille Pissarro and Georges Seurat, went even further with this way of painting. Sometimes they painted pictures made out of thousands of tiny dots of color. This way of painting is called **pointillism**. Try it yourself.

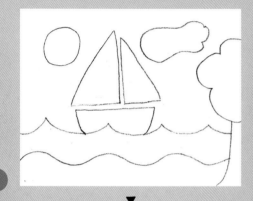

1. First, draw a simple outline of a place. Use the lines as guides, but do not be afraid to change your picture as you paint.

2. Mix colors you want to use on a palette. Dip a cotton swab into your paint. (Or, like Seurat and Pissarro, use the tips of your paintbrushes to make dots.)

3. Paint dots with the tip of the cotton swab. Try not to smear the dots together. Use a different cotton swab for each color you apply.

4. Experiment with color. You can make all kinds of new colors by placing different colored dots next to one another. I combined yellow dots with red and orange ones for my sun. I made a shimmering sky and water by placing dark and light blue dots side by side. Green and yellow dots together make a yellow-green treetop.

5. Cover the entire picture with dots. Look at your picture close up. Then step back from it and take a look. What do you notice? Seen from far away, your eyes blend the colors of the dots together.

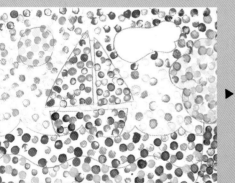

Supplies

Paper
Cotton swabs
Paint supplies

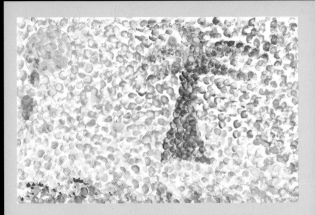

My desert island.—Julia, 12

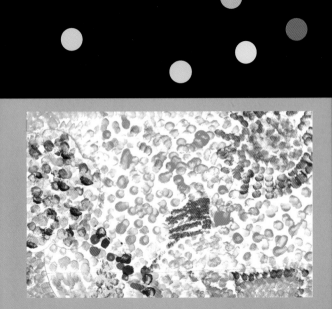

The flag flaps in the breeze.—Dylan, 12

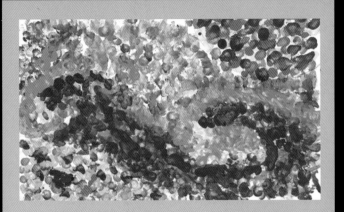

Look out for the wave!—Timothy, 11

This garden is wild.—Zeb, 9

Try this, too!

Make Abstract Art

The Impressionists inspired modern artists to paint in a new way. In **abstract painting**, you can capture the feeling and look of a place with colors and shapes. Instead of drawing details, freely paint colors that remind you of a place. For example, paint a wild garden with patches of greens and bright colors, or paint the movement of the ocean with swirling designs.

CITY SIGHTS

CAMILLE PISSARRO

In early February of 1897, Camille Pissarro moved into a hotel room in Paris, where he stayed for a few weeks. He set up his paints and easel near his window. Down below, he saw a busy street, the Boulevard Montmartre. Pissarro looked out the window day and night, and he painted fourteen pictures of this lively scene. As you can see, he captured the movement of the crowds strolling and the carriages traveling down the road.

Pissarro noticed that every day the street looked different, depending on the weather and the time of day or night. On the cold winter morning in this picture, he painted bare trees and a chilly gray sky. At other times, he showed people walking under umbrellas in the pouring rain or running down the street in a snowstorm. As the seasons passed from winter to spring, Pissarro painted the warm sky and the blossoming trees that lined the sidewalks. Look out your window. What do you see?

Take a stroll down this city street. Look around.
What would it be like to be in this picture?

- **Where** is this scene? How would you describe this **place**?
- What is the **weather** like? What **season** is it? What in the picture tells you that?
- Notice all of the **people**. What are they **doing**? Where do you think they are **going**?
- What kinds of **transportation** do you see? Can you tell in what direction the **traffic** is moving? What else seems to be **moving**?
- **Imagine**. If you were in this picture, how would you **feel**? What kinds of **sounds** would you hear in this place?

18

- Is this scene happening **now or a long time ago**? How can you tell?
- Pissarro painted this place at **different times**. Picture this place in springtime. What would be different about it? What would it look like at night?

Compare this place with the one in Monet's picture on page 9. Which one would you rather be in? Why?

The Boulevard Montmartre on a Winter Morning, 1897
oil on canvas, 25½ x 32 inches
The Metropolitan Museum of Art, New York

Have you ever visited a big city? Do you live in one?
Paint the excitement and beauty of the city.

Painting the Town

Make a city picture that captures the weather.
Did you ever visit the city during a snowstorm? The snow swirls in a flurry of movement and all the streets turn white. On rainy days, everything looks gray. I like when the sun is out and the sky is clear and bright. Like Pissarro, paint a city scene that captures the feeling of weather.

1. Watch the weather. Think about the kind of weather and season you want to show in your street scene. Is it a rainy gray day, a winter blizzard, or a bright spring day?

2. Cut sponges into shapes for your city. Pissarro painted his city scenes with paintbrushes, but you can also paint with sponges. Rectangular sponges can be used to make tall buildings. Triangular sponges can be rooftops. Cut other sponge shapes for the street, windows, cars, and anything else.

3. Mix colors you want to use. Spread the paint onto your palette or plate. Then dip a sponge into the paint. (Tip: Keep the paint thick for best results.)

4. Stamp it out! Press the sponge onto your paper. You can start by making a street. Then add a skyline of buildings.

5. *Swoosh!* Paint the sky. It's raining! It's pouring! Smear paint with your sponges to create the look of rain, snow, or wind in the sky. Drip or flick paint from a brush for raindrops or snow. Mix cool blues, purples, and white for a winter sky. You can also paint a dark night sky, a fiery sunset, or a bright blue sunny day.

6. What's on the street? Paint cars, trucks, people, windows, doors, or trees. Like Pissarro, you can make people and cars look blurry as if they are moving. If you like, use a paintbrush for details.

Supplies

Paper
Sponges
Brushes
Paint supplies

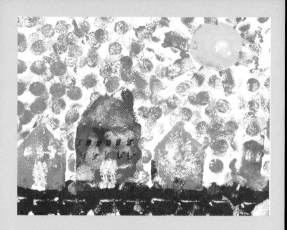

A sunny spring day.—Peter, 8

A stormy night.—Amanda, 8

Snow day!—Aviva, 10

The city blossoms in spring.—Aviva, 10

Try this, too!

Sunset Skyline

Have you ever seen how beautiful the city skyline looks when the sun is setting? Sometimes the sky turns orange and red. Buildings become dark shapes and the lights in the windows begin to shine. You can make a sunset sky by smearing warm colors (yellows, oranges, and reds) with your sponges. Then cut building shapes out of construction paper and glue them down. Paint or glue on windows, cars, smoke, and other finishing touches.

Sunset in the busy city.—Alyssa, 8

City Lights

Paint a city scene that shows day or night using watercolor resist.
Pissarro noticed how beautiful the city looks at different times. In early morning, he painted the mist on the street as the sun rose. At night, he showed the glittering city lights shining in the dark. Did you ever notice how spectacular the city looks in the evening when hundreds of lights sparkle, or how lively it is in the middle of the day?

1. Draw your own city using oil pastels or crayons. You can draw tall buildings, bridges, windows, traffic, people, trains, streetlights, and anything else you might see. (Tip: Press hard!)

2. What time is it? For a night scene, use light and white oil pastels to show the glistening lights of the windows or bridges. Add a moon and stars in the sky. Or draw the city by day with a sun shining.

3. Paint over the lines with watercolor. Let the paint flow freely through your picture. Notice how the crayon shows through and "resists" the watercolor. For a night scene, try dark colors such as purples and blues. For a day scene, you can use bright colors.

4. Same scene, different time. Make a second painting that shows the same place at a different time, day or night.

Supplies

Paper
Oil pastels or crayons
Watercolor paints
Brushes

Do not proceed according to rules and principles, but paint what you observe and feel.
—Camille Pissarro

Sunrise over the Statue of Liberty!
—Lance, 6

Stars shine at night.—Harold, 6

An afternoon rainbow!—Vanessa, 6

Try this, too!

Fun with Watercolor

Experiment with watercolor to create a city scene. Try **wet on wet** for the sky. Brush clean water onto your paper. Then apply wet watercolor paints to it, and watch it flow. You can even pick up your painting and tilt it back and forth to let the paint dip and swirl around the sky. Tap the end of your brush and let paint spatter for raindrops or stars. Paint in the buildings. Blend colors together. While your painting is still wet, sprinkle coarse salt onto it. Let it dry, then shake off the salt. You will get a dotted look that you can use for mist, snow, air, or light.

It's raining colors!—Aviva, 10

FIGURES IN MOTION

EDGAR DEGAS

The artist Edgar Degas was fascinated with the ballet. During his life, he made 600 artworks of dancers! Instead of painting the ballerinas' big performances, Degas mostly painted what went on behind the scenes during rehearsals and at dance class. In this picture, the girls are hard at work. Some seem tired or bored as they wait on the side. Each girl is shown in action. One is tying her shoe, another is scratching her back, and one seems to be yawning! In the center, a dancer twirls on her toes. Like a photograph, Degas's picture freezes the ballerinas' motions.

Degas visited the ballet often, and he made many sketches of the dancers. Later, in his studio, he worked from memory to plan his paintings carefully. Sometimes Degas took photographs to help him with his paintings.

Go behind the scenes. Watch the ballerinas.
What do you notice is happening?

- Who are these **girls**? What are they **doing**?
- Look at the **dancers** who are center stage. How would you describe the way they are **moving**?
- Notice the **man** in the middle of all the girls. **Who** could he be? What is he doing with his hands?
- Look at the girls around him. What is each one **doing**? How do you suppose they **feel**? Notice the one just to his left. Why is her **mouth open**? What might her arms be **reaching** for?
- Travel to the **back of the stage**. Who might those two men be?
- The name of this picture is *The Rehearsal Onstage*. What in the picture tells us the dancers are **practicing** and it is not the actual performance?

The Rehearsal Onstage, 1874
oil on canvas, 25½ x 32 inches
The Metropolitan Museum of Art, New York

- Like a photograph, this painting captures a **moment in time**. What kinds of movements are "frozen" in this picture?
- Look closely. Can you find something in the picture that tells you what kind of **music** they might be dancing to?
- Look at the edges of the picture. Notice the way the scene is cut off. If this scene kept going, what else might you **see** in this **place**?

If you could turn this picture on like a movie, what would happen next?

Do you study dance or play a sport? The art projects in this section invite you to capture yourself in motion.

People on the Move

Try pastels, like Degas

Draw yourself in motion, playing a sport, dancing, or doing another action.

In Degas's picture, the movement of each dancer is frozen. Some ballerinas twirl on their toes and others prepare for their rehearsal. Degas made hundreds of paintings, sketches, and pastel drawings to study the way dancers move. Make your own drawing that captures you in motion.

1. Experiment with pastels. Make different lines: Use the side of the pastel or the tip. Press hard or soft. Layer colors on top of one another. Blend them together with a paper towel. Try crosshatching: Make many lines in one direction, then draw over them in another direction with another color. Try these in your drawing.

2. Picture yourself in motion. For example, pose as if you are about to shoot a basketball into a hoop. Or pretend you are skating on ice or dancing like a ballerina. Look in the mirror to see your body, or just imagine what you look like.

3. Draw yourself with simple shapes. Sketch lightly. You can make a rectangle for the body and an oval for the head. Then draw the movement of the arms and legs. Are you reaching up into the air like a cheerleader or bending your legs as you run?

4. Add clothing and details. Are you wearing a tutu, a skating outfit, or a sports uniform? Use the tip of the pastel for details such as the face, hands, and feet.

5. Show movement. Smudge the pastels to make your drawing blurry, as if you are in motion. You can also draw sweeping lines to get the feeling of clothes or hair moving.

6. Draw the setting. Are you onstage, at a skating rink, or on a basketball court? Like Degas, you can also draw the audience or people who are watching the event. (When you are finished, ask an adult to spray your picture with hair spray or pastel fixative to prevent smearing.)

Supplies

Pastel paper
Pastels

Go, team, go!—Cindy, 10

Play ball!—Jacob, 10

I love ice skating!—Kaitlyn, 9

Try these, too!

Capture It—One, Two, Three

Sometimes Degas drew the same dancer over and over again on one sheet of paper to show her as she moved. Like Degas, make a drawing that shows a person in motion in three different positions. For example, you might show a basketball player dribbling the ball, running, and shooting for the hoop.

He shoots, he scores!—Isaac, 9

It's a Snap!

Take photos that show people in motion or collect pictures from magazines that show people in action. For example, find a photo of a hockey player skating or a skier shooting down a mountain. Or take your own photo of a friend jumping or doing a cartwheel. Paste your pictures on a large piece of paper or posterboard to make a photo-collage.

Action Figures

Make a sculpture, like Degas

Sculpt a person in motion using plaster gauze.

As Degas grew older, he began to lose his eyesight. He worked with his hands to create sculptures of dancers in different poses, stretching or twirling. One of his most famous works is a statue of a fourteen-year-old ballerina. He dressed it with a real tutu, a hair ribbon, and ballet slippers. He even added a wig made of real hair! Make your own sculpture of a person in motion and dress it up.

1. Make a "stick figure" out of 12-inch pipe cleaners or wire. Bend a loop for the head and twist the ends of the pipe cleaner for the body. Then twist on arms and legs. Bend your wire figure into a pose that shows an activity. You can make a dancer, a skater, a surfer, or anyone you like.

2. Cover it with aluminum foil. Mold the foil around the wire to form your person in motion.

3. Cut the plaster gauze into small strips, each about 1 inch wide and 2 inches long. Cut smaller pieces for details.

4. Wrap your person. Dunk a plaster gauze strip into warm water. Gently squeeze off excess water. Piece by piece, wrap the entire person with plaster gauze. Then give it a second layer.

5. Let your figure dry overnight, then paint it.

6. Dress it up. Collect materials from your home. Glue on yarn or tissue paper for hair. Make a skirt by scrunching up tissue paper. Decorate it with jewels, beads, or ribbons. Add objects such as a skateboard, a ball, or a bouquet of flowers. You can glue on wiggly eyes or sequins for eyes.

Supplies

Pipe cleaners
Foil
Plaster gauze (buy at craft store or surgical supply store)
Water
Scissors
Paint supplies
Glue
Decorative materials

I caught the bouquet! —Zoe, 7

Skater dude! —David A., 7

I play soccer. —David M., 7

Try these, too!

Animals in Action

Degas also made many sculptures, sketches, and paintings that show horses in motion. Make a sculpture that shows an animal moving. Create a running cat or a galloping horse. Add whiskers, a tail, a collar, and other details out of materials you collect.

Running fox. —Lindsey, 7

Set the Stage

Create a place for your figures—for example, you can make a stage for your ballerina or a ballfield for a baseball player. Start with a box. Paint or paste down materials such as paper curtains or fake grass for the floor and background. Invite your friends to make other members of the team or more ballerinas, then arrange them in the setting.

Everyone claps for me! —Cosima, 7

Changing Faces Another Degas idea

Capture a facial expression in a painting.

What does your face look like when you are sleeping, eating, or laughing? How do you look when you are surprised or sad or angry? Instead of painting only smiling faces, Degas painted all kinds of facial expressions. In his pictures, you can see people yawning or singing. You can also tell how they feel.

1. Make different faces as you look in the mirror. Or play this game with friends. Choose a facial expression—sleeping, winking, eating, yawning—or a feeling such as sad, happy, angry, surprised, or scared. Act it out with your face. See if your friends can guess what you are trying to show.

2. Sketch your face. Start with a large oval for the head. Then add facial features and details such as eyes, mouth, nose, ears, and hair.

3. Draw a mouth in action—doing something. A circle or oval will show an open mouth screaming, yawning, eating, or surprised. A mouth with big teeth might show anger. A downward curve might show a sad face pouting.

5. Make eyes that show an expression. Big circles for eyes might look surprised. Eyebrows pointed down will show anger. Closed eyes might show sleeping or singing.

6. Add other clues to show what the person is doing. If the person is eating, you can draw food. Draw musical notes for singing, or tears for crying.

7. Paint your face. Use the ideas in Colorful You, on opposite page, to help you mix skin colors.

Supplies

Paper
Brushes
Paint supplies

Copying what we see is all very well, but it is much better to draw what we remember.
—Edgar Degas

Sing with me!—Rachel, 8

I like to make silly faces.—Mary, 10

Oh no!—Candice, 8

Try this, too!

Colorful You!

Experiment with mixing different skin colors. Make light skin by mixing orange, white, and a touch of red. Brown skin can be made from blue and orange. Add white to make skin lighter. Mix in red to show rosy cheeks. Add a touch of blue to your colors to make skin darker or duller. How many skin colors can you create?

So sad.—Aubri, 8

CELEBRATIONS
PIERRE-AUGUSTE RENOIR

Pierre-Auguste Renoir wanted to paint Moulin, an outdoor garden near his home in Paris where people danced. His friends helped him carry his huge canvas—measuring about 4 feet high and 6 feet wide—onto the dance floor. He set up his easel right there and painted the lively activity he saw around him. Later he added the finishing touches at home.

Like a snapshot, Renoir's painting captures people in action having fun. Everyone seems to be having a good time, dancing and talking. The women are all dressed up in pretty gowns that swirl as they dance. The men wear top hats or straw boater hats, the fashion of the day. Sunlight flickers through the trees in this merry outdoor festivity. Some people did not like Renoir's painting because they thought it looked messy. Others admired Renoir's joyful pictures, and he became known as "the painter of happiness."

Join the celebration. What would it be like to be in this scene?

- What do you think the people are **doing together**?
- There are many little **scenes** in this picture. Notice the group of **young men and women** at the front of the picture. What is each one **doing**? Who seems to be **talking** to whom? Notice their eyes. What do you suppose each one is **looking at**?
- Look at the people **dancing**. What kind of **music** might they be listening to? What other **sounds** might you hear in this picture?
- Travel around the picture. Can you find someone who is **sitting** on a bench? Can you find someone **leaning against a tree**? What might they be thinking, or doing there? What else do you see?
- How many **children** can you find? What are they doing?
- Look carefully. Which people in the picture seem to be **moving**?

Dance at the Moulin de la Galette, 1876
oil on canvas, 51 x 69 inches
Musée d'Orsay, Paris

- Where is this taking **place**? Is it **inside or outside**? How can you tell? What kind of **occasion** might this be?
- Is this scene happening **now or a long time ago**? What in the picture tells you?
- **Imagine**. . .what would it be like to be in this **crowd**? Would it be **fun**? Why or why not?

Compare this dance painting to Degas's picture on page 25. Which would you rather be in? Why?

What kind of celebrations do you enjoy?
The art projects in this section invite you to paint pictures of your good times and happiness.

Outdoor Festivities

Make a picture that shows an outdoor celebration with paint and collage.

Renoir loved to paint scenes of people enjoying themselves outdoors. In his painting of Moulin, you can see the sunlight flickering through the trees as the people dance and frolic in the garden dance hall. Like Renoir, paint a *fête galante*—French for "a fun outside amusement."

1. What do you celebrate outdoors? Here are some ideas: the Fourth of July, a pool party, a picnic, a barbeque, a birthday party, a wedding.

2. Make the place. You can paint it, like Renoir. Or cut and paste paper shapes—grass, trees, clouds—to create the setting. Fill your picture with things you need for the party. Make a table, chairs, a sun umbrella, a picnic blanket, a pool, a volleyball, or anything else.

3. Paint over your cut-paper shapes. Use quick brushstrokes for the sky and dabs of color for trees and a garden in bloom.

4. Add people. Like Renoir, you can put many people in the picture doing different things. Some might be eating, talking, dancing, or resting. Dress them up for the occasion. (Use a small brush or draw the details.)

5. Show what they are celebrating. Add balloons and presents for a birthday party. An American flag and fireworks show the Fourth of July. Don't forget the food or special cake for your celebration!

Supplies

Colored paper
Scissors
Glue
Brushes
Paint supplies

Why shouldn't art be pretty?
—Pierre-Auguste Renoir

It's very romantic.—Allison, 11

They're getting married.—Erika, 10

July 4th pool party!—Anthony, 11

Sunshine girl!—Nicole, 10

Try this, too!

Outdoor Portraits

Renoir painted portraits of people outside in beautiful settings. In some of his paintings, you can see children in colorful gardens surrounded by flowers. He showed the sunlight as it filtered through the trees and warmed their skin. Paint a picture of yourself in a garden or another outdoor spot. Make different greens for the leaves by mixing yellows, blues, and whites. Paint spots of color for flowers and the rays of the sun.

Let's Dance

Capture the movement of your favorite dance in a painting.
Look at the people dancing in Renoir's painting. The couples seem to be in motion as they dance. The women's long dresses sway, and the lively brushstrokes and colors seem to move across the picture. What kind of dancing do you enjoy? Paint a picture of it.

▼

1. Freeze dance! Pose as if you are dancing. Or play music and move to it. Notice how your body is moving. Are your arms in the air? Are your feet kicking up?

2. Draw simple lines to show people dancing. Start with an oval for the head and a shape for the body. Then draw lines to show the movement of the legs and arms. I drew a man and woman holding hands as they swing dance. For break dancing, draw someone upside down or doing a flip. For a ballerina, draw her leg pointed in the air as she spins.

3. Dress them up! Paint costumes for the dance they are doing. A break dancer might wear a T-shirt and jeans. A ballerina wears a tutu. A lady at a ball is dressed in a fancy gown.

4. Make it move. Use sweeping brushstrokes to show the movement of the dance. I painted quick brushstrokes to show the girl's dress swirling as she spins. Her hair is flowing in the air and her necklace is swaying.

5. Paint the place with lively brushstrokes. Use lines to show the direction of movement. You can also show where it is taking place—at a party, in the city, on a stage, or outside.

▼

Supplies

Paper
Brushes
Paint supplies

by Alex, 12

36

Rockettes! —Jaclyn, 12

The tango.—Paula, 11

Break dancing!—Ricky, 12

Making Music

Renoir celebrated music, and he loved to make portraits of people playing musical instruments. In one of his famous paintings, he showed a beautiful girl playing the piano. In another, he painted a girl with her violin. Do you play a musical instrument? Make a portrait of yourself or someone else playing a musical instrument you love.

The clarinet is cool!—Gabrielle, 9

FAMILY PICTURES

MARY CASSATT

Mary Cassatt's favorite subject was women and their children. She painted families the way they look naturally—doing everyday things together. Like a snapshot, Cassatt's paintings freeze a passing moment in time. In her pictures, you can see a mom as she kisses her child or gives her baby a bath. In this painting, a mother sits outside with her children. Feel the warm sunlight filtering through the trees onto their faces. You can see the love between them. Notice the way the mother tenderly looks down at her baby. Her hands hold the chubby belly firmly. The baby reaches for his older sister's face. It is up to us to imagine what they are thinking and feeling.

Cassatt did not have children of her own. She devoted herself to painting the special closeness that mothers and children share. For Cassatt, art was a wonderful adventure, and she explored many ways of making pictures.

Take a close look at this family. What does this picture tell you about them?

- Who might these **people** be? What are they **doing together**?
- Who is the **woman**? How do you think she feels about the **children**? What do you notice about the way she is holding the **baby**?
- Look at the children. Notice the way the girl is looking at the baby. How do you think she **feels**? What might she be **thinking**?
- What is the girl holding in her **hand**? Why do you think she has this?
- How would you **describe** the baby? Why do you think the baby is **reaching**?
- What else do you notice about these people?

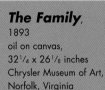

The Family,
1893
oil on canvas,
32¼ x 26⅛ inches
Chrysler Museum of Art,
Norfolk, Virginia

- Can you tell **where** they are? Follow the path to the back of the picture. What do you see there?
- Mary Cassatt often painted women and children in a **loving moment**. What shows love in this picture? What other feeling do you think this picture expresses?

Who would you paint in your **family picture**? What would you put in your picture to show you **love one another**?

What do you do with your family?
Make paintings, prints, photographs, and drawings that capture life in your family.

Me and My Mom or Dad

Make art inspired by Cassatt

Draw a picture that shows what you do with your mom, dad, or other family members in your everyday life.

Rather than painting families during special occasions such as holidays or birthdays, Cassatt painted what families do together every day. In her paintings, she showed mothers with their children—giving a baby a bath, taking a nap together, or sitting outside. These kinds of pictures about everyday life are called **genre scenes**.

1. What do you do with your mother or father every day? Maybe you shop together, watch television, play sports, or eat a meal together.

2. Capture a loving moment in your picture. I drew my father singing me a lullaby at bedtime when I was a little girl. Maybe your mom or dad reads you a story before you go to sleep, or maybe you play games together.

3. Draw the people. Sketch simple outlines. Start with an oval for the head, then add the body, arms, and legs. Show what they are doing.

4. Where is it? Draw the setting. I drew a cozy pink bedroom. Look out the window. You can tell it is night because I drew stars and a moon.

5. Add details to tell the story. My father is singing "Over the Rainbow." I drew musical notes, a rainbow, and an open mouth to show that. What will you put in your picture?

6. Color it. You can create many different colors with colored pencils or crayons. Draw over one color with another one. For example, draw blue over pink to get a purplish color. You can also press hard or soft to get different kinds of lines and shades.

Supplies

Paper
Colored pencils or crayons

My mother sings lullabies.—Alessandra, 11

We go to the mall together.—Arielle, 12

Dad builds models with me.—Ian, 10

Try this, too!

Everyday Memories

Photograph a day in the life of your family. Take snapshots of everyday things you do together—watching television, getting ready for school, eating a meal, playing together, or bedtime. Put your pictures in a family journal. Write stories and captions about them. (Remember, it is polite to ask people before you take their pictures.)

In the evening, after I wash my hair, my mother brushes it. Then I do my home-work. After that, I play a game with my brother. We all have dessert while we watch TV.—Raquel, 8, and her brothers, Timmy, 10, Ray, 12, and Kevin, 13

Baby Me

More Cassatt ideas

Make a portrait of yourself as a baby using paint and pastels.

Cassatt loved to experiment with new ways of making art. Sometimes she drew over her paintings with pastels. Try it yourself. Like Cassatt, make a baby **portrait** with paint and pastels that shows the love between mother and child. (A portrait is an artwork of a real person.)

1. Picture yourself as a baby. How did your mom, dad, or other adult take care of you? Maybe your mother held you in her arms and rocked you to sleep. Maybe your father wrapped you in a blanket and made funny faces at you. Maybe your grandparent fed you a bottle or sang you a song.

2. Draw an outline of the people. Sketch lightly, and draw big shapes. You can draw a circle for the baby's face and an oval for the grown-up. Then draw in the bodies. Show what they are doing. For example, if you want the people to be hugging, draw the arms reaching across to one another.

3. Paint the colors of the faces, clothes, and the background first. Draw in the details, such as the facial features, later.

4. Let the paint dry. Then color back over it with pastel. Sketch in clouds, trees, and grass. Use the side of the pastels for large areas. Blend and mix colors. Draw with the tip of the pastel for details of the face and hands. (As you work, do not lean on your picture—it will smudge. When you are finished, ask an adult to spray the picture with hair spray or pastel fixative to prevent smearing.)

Supplies

Paper
Paint supplies
Paintbrushes
Pastels

I love to paint children. They are so natural and truthful.—Mary Cassatt

by Kristen, 11

See my rattle?—Amy, 12

Here I am taking my first steps.
—Allen, 11

Try this, too!

Wet Pastels
Did you know that if you get pastels wet, they turn into paint? Draw a picture with pastels. Then gently wipe areas of your drawing with a wet paintbrush. Notice how the dry pastels become watery colors. Then you can draw back into your picture again. Or start by crushing your pastels and mixing water with them to make a paste to paint with.

I'm on top of an anthill!
—Eric, 10

I'm waving bye-bye.
—Maxine, 11

Printing Portraits

Another Cassatt idea

Make a family portrait using plastic-foam printing.
In addition to painting, Cassatt and her friends Edgar Degas and Camille Pissarro explored the art of printmaking. (A **print** is made when you make a copy of your artwork.) The kinds of prints that Cassatt made—etchings, aquatints, and drypoint—require special chemicals and a printing press. This project shows you a simple printmaking method that you can do at home.

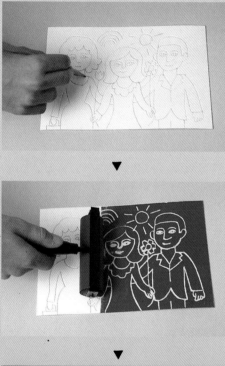

1. Make the printing plate. You can buy plastic-foam (often called Styrofoam) sheets from an art supply store, or cut a flat rectangle out of a disposable plastic-foam plate or a clean meat-packing tray.

2. Press lines into the plastic foam with a pencil. Notice how the lines are actually carved into the sheet. (If you press too lightly, your picture will not show up.) Draw simple shapes and lines; details that are too tiny will not work. Do not write words—they will print backward.

3. Roll ink onto the printing plate with a brayer (roller). Start at the top, and roll carefully. Try to get an even coat of ink. Notice how the lines show up white! (Tip: Do not put too much ink on your brayer—it will fill up the lines.)

4. Place a sheet of paper over the printing plate. Gently rub and press with your hand or a clean brayer.

5. Surprise! Lift up the paper to see your print.

6. Copy it! Repeat the process to print more pictures. Experiment. Roll out more than one color ink and make a rainbow print. Try printing on different types of papers. How many different looks can you get from the same picture?

Supplies

Water-based
 printing ink
Brayer (roller)
Paper
Pencil
Plastic-foam sheet

My dog is like family!—Amber, 8

Me and my uncle.—Aura, 9

Twin sisters.—Aubri, 8

I play football.—Jonathan, 9

Try this, too!

Press It Out

Pissarro and Degas made prints by applying ink or paint to a flat metal surface. Then they pressed paper against the metal and ran it through a printing press. Experiment. Get a disposable plastic plate. Turn it over and make a painting on the back. Keep the paint or ink thick and work quickly. Then press a sheet of paper over your painting and lift it up. A one-of-a-kind print like this is called a **monotype**. After the picture dries (or even before), you can draw back into your printed picture with pastel.

Artist Biographies

Claude Monet
French, 1840–1926

Claude Monet was born in Paris. He grew up in northern France in a port by the sea called Le Havre. As a boy, Monet drew pictures of his teachers and friends and sketched outdoors at the harbor. When he was eighteen, Monet moved to Paris to study art.

He became friends with artists who loved to paint outdoors. They took trips to the forest and along the river Seine and painted what they saw outside. Monet even built an art studio aboard a little boat so he could paint as he floated down the river. He worked quickly with bright colors to capture the changing sunlight and weather.

Monet faced many difficult times. During the Franco-Prussian War, he fled to London. A year later, he returned to France and moved to Argenteuil. A few years later, his wife died. No matter what happened, he continued to paint. Most of Monet's paintings were rejected from the important art exhibition called the Salon. In 1874, he and his friends decided to hold their own show. But no one bought his art, and he was poor.

Monet began painting scenes of the French seaside, and finally his paintings began to sell. He remarried, and he moved to a house on the river in a town called Giverny. There he created a magnificent garden that inspired beautiful paintings. Today, Monet is known as one of the world's greatest artists, and his home in Giverny is a museum.

Camille Pissarro
French, 1830–1903

Camille Pissarro was born on the island of St. Thomas, where his family owned a business. His family was Jewish, originally from France and Portugal, and included many artists. As a boy, Pissarro mostly taught himself to draw and paint because there was not much art instruction available on St. Thomas.

When Pissarro was in his twenties, he moved to Venezuela. He painted country people and the outdoors. Later, he settled in Paris, where he studied painting at the School of Fine Arts and copied masterpieces at the Louvre museum. He became friends with Impressionist artists who, like him, painted outside with bright colors. Later in his life, he lived in the country, in Pontoise, with his wife and eight children. He loved to paint the beauty of the countryside, but he also painted the busy streets of Paris. Sometimes he painted in a pointillist style, with tiny dots of color. He also explored watercolor and printmaking.

Pissarro's paintings were accepted into the important exhibition, the Salon, but his paintings did not sell. In 1874, he helped organize the first Impressionist exhibition. Even though at times he was poor, he was generous and willing to help younger artists. At the end of his life, his work began to sell. Today, Pissarro is sometimes called the "father of Impressionism."

Edgar Degas
French, 1834–1917

Edgar Degas was born into a wealthy family in Paris, where he lived most of his life. As a boy, Degas visited the city's opera and museums and took art classes. Degas wanted to be an artist, but his father disagreed and sent him to law school. Later, Degas left to study painting at the School of Fine Arts. He also copied masterpieces in museums. He traveled to Italy, London, and the United States, painting everywhere he went.

Degas began painting people and animals in motion. He went to the racetrack and sketched the horses. He visited the opera and ballet and studied the movements of the performers. Rather than painting the big event, Degas painted what went on during practice. Degas also painted people doing everyday things such as working or combing their hair.

Degas became friends with Impressionist artists in Paris who, like him, wanted to capture a moment in time in their pictures. Degas, however, did not go outside with his friends to paint. He always painted inside his studio. In 1874, Degas helped organize the first Impressionist exhibition. At first, many people did not like his paintings. Later, his paintings of ballerinas began to sell, and he became famous. Degas also made pastels, prints, and photographs. When he grew old and began to lose his eyesight, he created sculptures and bright pastels. Today, he is known as a leader of Impressionism.

Pierre-Auguste Renoir
French, 1841–1919

When Pierre-Auguste Renoir was three, his family moved to Paris, where he lived most of his life. As a boy, Renoir visited the city's museum, the Louvre, and copied masterpieces. When he was thirteen, he got a job painting decorations on cups and plates. As a young man, he went to the School of Fine Arts to study painting seriously.

Renoir became friends with other artists in Paris who, like him, painted outdoors. They took trips to the countryside and painted what they saw outside. He and Monet went to a popular boating spot, Le Grenouillère, and painted side by side. Renoir painted people enjoying themselves at dances and parties, in the city and in the country. He painted joyful scenes of beautiful women relaxing by the river or in the garden. Soft light flickers through trees, and flowers burst with color.

Many of Renoir's colorful paintings were rejected from the Salon, the important exhibition in Paris. In 1874, Renoir and his friends decided to hold their own art exhibition. At first, many people disliked Renoir's art. But then, when Renoir began painting portraits of wealthy families, his work began to sell. Renoir married and had three sons. He loved children and painted them playing with toys. Renoir is known as the "painter of happiness" and is a leader of Impressionism.

Mary Cassatt
American, 1845–1926

Mary Cassatt was born in Pittsburgh, Pennsylvania, into a wealthy family. When she was seven, her family moved to Paris, France. As a child, she visited the city's great art museums. Cassatt wanted to be an artist, but at first her family disapproved. Later, her family returned to the United States, and she attended the Pennsylvania Academy of Fine Arts. As a young woman, she moved to Paris to study art.

Cassatt's paintings were accepted into the Salon, the important exhibition in Paris. She became a successful artist and traveled around Europe. When she returned to Paris, she became close friends with Edgar Degas. They explored new ways of making art with pastels and printmaking. Degas invited her to join the Impressionist artists, and she participated in their exhibitions.

Cassatt's paintings capture mothers and children in everyday life. In her pictures, you can see mothers hugging their babies or giving them baths. When Cassatt's mother, father, and sister came to live with her in Paris, she painted her family doing ordinary things such as drinking tea or relaxing in the garden.

Long ago, when Cassatt lived, most women were not permitted to study art and to sell their paintings. Women were expected to raise children and take care of the home. Cassatt did not marry and have children. She devoted herself to painting pictures that show the love between mother and child. Today, Cassatt is considered a great Impressionist artist.

by *Emma, 11*

About the Author

Joyce Raimondo, creator of the Art Explorers series, is director of Imagine That! Art Education, specializing in helping children access the arts. As a visiting author to schools and consultant, she teaches children how to look at famous artworks and use art history as a springboard for their own creativity. Her clients have included *Blue's Clues*, the Children's Television Workshop, and the Pollock-Krasner House and Study Center, among others.

Joyce and Buddy

She is author of The Museum of Modern Art's acclaimed Art Safari series of children's books, kits, and online program. From 1992–2000, she served as family programs coordinator at MoMA in New York, where she created programs that teach children and adults how to enjoy art.

A painter and sculptor, Joyce Raimondo's illustrations have been featured in such publications as *The New York Times* and *The Boston Globe*. Her television appearances include *Blue's Clues, Fox Breakfast Time,* and *NBC News,* among others. She divides her time between Manhattan and Amagansett, New York. Visit her on the web at www.joyceraimondo.com.

Acknowledgments

As director of Imagine That! Art Education, I implement workshops designed to teach children how to enjoy art history. I ask students to describe what they see in famous artworks and follow up with their own creations. Much of the children's art featured in this book was made during these workshops.

A special thanks go to the children who contributed artworks: Joseph, Dezaray, Victoria, Paula, Jaclyn, Bradley, Natalia, Jeannette, Alison, Travis, Melaina, Maria, Shannon, Allison M., Julie, Anthony, Christina, Julia, Dylan, Timothy, Zeb, Peter, Amanda, Aviva, Alyssa, Lance, Vanessa, Cindy, Kaitlyn, Jacob, Allison D., Isaac, David M., Zoe, David A., Cosima, Lindsey, Rachel, Candice, Aubri, Erika, Anthony, Nicole, Ricky, Gabrielle, Alex, Alessandra, Arielle, Ian, Raquel, Timmy, Ray, Kevin, Amy, Allen, Maxine, Eric, Kristen, Amber, Aura, Jonathan, Allison E., and Emma.

Gratitude is given to my editors, Julie Mazur and Laaren Brown, for bringing clarity to the development of the second volume in the Art Explorers series. I am also thankful to Ed Miller, the designer, for creating the book's lively graphics.

Grateful acknowledgment is due to the institutions who participated in this project: Amagansett School, Brooklyn Avenue School, Chestnut Hill Elementary, Project Most (East Hampton), Springs School, and Woodward Parkway Elementary. I am especially thankful to the administrators and art teachers who welcomed me to their schools: MaryJane Aceri, Bruce Alster, Jane Berzner, Tim Bryden, Nancy Carney, Elizabeth Clint, Rebbecca Morgan, Linda Rudes, Eleanor Tritt, and Ricki Weisfelner. Appreciation is given to the Nassau and Suffolk Boards of Cooperative Education who funded many of these workshops and to the coordinators, Pam Steffner, Lori Horowitz, and Laura Muhs, who arranged them.